LITTLE GIRL CAN DANCE
THE TALE OF ANDROMEDA TOLD IN SIX SMASHING MOVEMENTS

TRICIA D. WAGNER

LYRIDAE BOOKS

PRAISE FOR TRICIA D. WAGNER

I believe art is utterly important.
It's one of the things that could save us.

Mary Oliver

Andromeda, more beautiful than angels of the sea.
Andromeda, a blush of galaxy.
Andromeda, Queen of Starry Night's fair child.

Andromeda, forsaken by the Constellation King.
Andromeda, cast to the beasty thing.
Andromeda, ruler of men.

Andromeda, wellspring of the dragon and the dame.
Andromeda, maiden bound to rock with chain.
Andromeda, true to your own worth.

To you, this is my tribute.

I

Andromeda glances across the backyard toward the kitchen window.

The glass is dark, but still—Grandmother might be watching.

Andromeda lifts her teacup the way it's done if you're filthy rich, fingers reeking of dollars, the teacup itself costing a father's fortune.

"These gardens on the Isle of Messina are nothing short of spectacular," she says faux posh, like Grandmother.

The creature Blunder hums from across a table clustered with delicacies, tight as the grapes overgrowing Grandmother's garage; corpulent savories like what they ate at the reveling in Grandmother's Shakespearean play.

There are rare cuts of beef, and flutes of white wine, and cheeses torn, and croissants steaming warm.

Andromeda straightens to pull off what Grandmother calls *bien comfaits*— "well-behaved." Her foot won't stop the tapping that grates Grandmother's nerves, but that's fine. If she's watching, she can't see beneath the folds of this empire summer dress.

The truth is—Andromeda can pull off an excellent Hero, like in *Much Ado About Nothing*, casting shy glances. If Grandmother just would look out here, she might change her mind.

"I want a goodbye," says the creature Blunder, spectacular fangs overflowing his underbite.

"I hate goodbyes." Andromeda manages the Tuscan Isle accent perfectly. "So do you."

Blunder swipes away his platter of victuals. "You're no lady."

The creature Blunder seems not to be having a nice evening. He heard Grandmother say that Andromeda's beyond her control; that boarding school is the only machine that can fix her.

Andromeda pounds the table so hard that a basket of napkins goes flying. "I'm a jewel!"

A shade crosses inside the dark kitchen window.

Andromeda snatches her teacup and cradles it. "Creatures are rarely invited to reveling luncheons, you know."

'Luncheon,' another word belonging to Grandmother. It has the right sort of feel, but it stinks of pimento and cauliflower. Andromeda sips tea and tries to think of a better one.

Blunder taps his claws on the table. He, too, seems at a loss for words.

"Keep singing," she orders him.

Blunder sets into warbling—a mockery of the lullaby sung in that Shakespearean play, ending in everyone dancing. The melody is pleasing, though Blunder keeps having to suck breaths, hunching, as he must to approximate lady-like sitting. (His spiked tail curled beneath isn't at all helping things.)

"Sweet creature. You sing like a nightingale." Andromeda presses the petal-thin rim of her cup to her lips, but not too firmly. Pressing it too hard, even to her full, lady lips, might crack it.

"Here's to the sunniest summer, to lots of white petals falling from trees in Messina, and to excellent dancing." She clinks her cup to the claw Blunder reaches.

He lifts his song to a loftier key.

She offers her most pleasing smile. "Looking at you ruins the magic of the evening some."

Blunder's singing turns to a snarl. No wonder Grandmother pretends not to see him.

The sun paints silver on the sea-swollen clouds and shoots out, limelight fashion.

"How can I be anything but honest when the summer sun spotlighting our veranda (what's a veranda?) is piercing us to the soul, and making our hair shine, and our teeth?" She bares her teeth, most of them all-the-way-in lady-teeth.

In the kitchen window, the shadow stops. Grandmother is watching.

Her eyes and Andromeda's catch.

Grandmother's face, barely visible through the dinged window seems an odd compilation of regret and relief.

Grandmother backs into the darkness. Her silhouette fades.

Blunder sets his scaly paws on the table, leans in, and roars, showing all his teeth, so much whiter and sharper than Andromeda's.

"Fine, don't pretend!" She hurls her cup through his head.

The cup bounces down a stone path and strikes the trunk of a spruce.

It comes to rest on a scattering of needles and lies dully in the choked twilight. It's no longer a teacup, but just a pinecone.

Blunder points his claw at her. "Your mom taught you no manners."

"I haven't got any mom!"

The declaration shocks Blunder so bad that he vanishes in a puff of steam, leaving Andromeda alone and breathing hard, the evening fogging before her.

Andromeda's mom wasn't really a mom. Real moms want kids, and hers didn't. (Though, she might very well have if she'd known how this little girl can dance.)

Mom had been too young, Grandmother said, but she believed her lover—who wasn't really a lover—when he told her refusing kids was like avoiding the draft. So, Mom had a daughter and split, and the lover was bones in the earth, leaving the fruits of their dutiful deed to Grandmother.

Andromeda pictures her parents half-turning to see her from their dance floor, then vanishing.

She glances at the wide, shining sky, willing it to be a Messina countryside canopy.

But it fails. It isn't wide. Only tall neighbor's houses lean in. And nothing is shining. And everything's gray.

Quietly growling, Blunder crawls out of a puddle and ambles to her. He settles by her feet, sticks his back claw inside his huge ear and sets to digging.

The rain that threatened all afternoon falls.

Andromeda winks as drops strike her eyes. "Will you not play along, sky? This is it. My last chance."

Though the sky's bent on storming, it doesn't have Blunder's spunk, and it refuses to even growl its defiance. It just falls apart all over her until she's soaked.

Grandmother's golden patio bulbs—strung around the fence—zap awake in the artificial dusk of the storm.

"You've caught me," Andromeda shouts, spotlights—stage lights—all around, snapping on.

They turn toward her, as though cranked by an invisible gaffer.

And what can she do but take her place at the center of the stage?

Drills to begin with. First position. Second position. Third. Pirouette.

No, not ballet. Ballet's a poor pairing for this mud-splattery storm.

Tap dancing, then. The stone path is dotted with puddles and makes a smart catwalk.

She clickity clacks down and up it, her hands jazzy and cool. She taps until tapping with no music loses its novelty.

Interpretive dance, it must be.

This feels right. Interpretive dance needs no music, and there is no music because Blunder's refusing to sing and is just sitting by the teacup-turned-pinecone, sniveling.

Interpretive dancing needs every bit of the body. Andromeda conjures her finest prowl, moving along the fence to share the story of the tiger who spends his days pacing the length of the glass.

She scrambles from one end of the yard to the other, casting her arms at gate handles, trying each exit. But all are forbidden. Even the last gate, hanging open, is unpassable, strung as it is with Grandmother's decorative lights.

Though a boundary line, the lights are beautiful. Though beautiful, they are a boundary line.

Grandmother seems like a queen laying claim to all things wrapped inside of those lights—clothes to keep nice and a backyard for show and opinions for swallowing.

She claims even a little girl who doesn't belong to her, and the power to force the little girl to live at a boarding school for at-risk girls.

Andromeda lifts a long, smooth stick and holds it to one of the lights.

It brightly divides Grandmother's property from what doesn't belong to her—all that living city and wide world where her proclamations don't matter.

Andromeda swings.

The bulb bursts.

She waits for the flicker and snap of the whole line.

They don't fizzle, but just go on beaming their filaments, bright and defiant like tongues.

Another, better whack. Another bulb pops.

But the line doesn't die. The machine is too failsafe.

Andromeda roars at the sharp bulbs. Blunder comes alongside and roars with her.

Rain peppers her face and splatters off Blunder's blue scales.

The sky dims a degree, and not just because of the storm.

"Blunder, this is it. You must sing." She glances at the dark kitchen window.

Blunder sings, and Andromeda puts every lesson Grandmother gave her to work. Ballet, tap, jazz, free movement, interpretive dancing, line dancing—Shirley Temple suck on this—it all comes together in treacherous spirals, in sinister skulking against the fence, in gravity defying leaps, in baffling footwork, in graceful hands, in fingers held just so, the way dancers pose in Shakespearean movies.

"You call that dancing?" shouts a voice, from a hole in the fence. "Let's see what you've got."

"Get lost, Spike!" She hurls a pinecone at the hole.

It hits clean.

"Spike's not my name, and you know it."

It's true. Spike isn't his name.

But he was the one to find the dead dog in the alley.

It was long dead and soft as a fungus and covered in flies. She saw instantly that it was a zombie dog and likely to rise if they didn't blow it up.

He said it was not a zombie dog, because its brain would've rotted to nothing by now. Zombies require at least some bit of brain. And he should know because his dad performed neurosurgery.

She argued that it made no difference to the situation what his dad did for a living, and of course the dog still had a brain (it still had a body, didn't it?). It would rise with the blood moon. They had to blow it up.

They squared off at an impasse, no arguments left. And so, they did the only thing to do. They cleared off the flies and carried the dead dog on a cardboard sheet into his house for the surgery.

The best way to get at the brain pan was through the eye, he said, and luckily, right there, by the dumpster, they found a railroad spike.

They laid the dog on his dining room table, which he said was a place very much like the operating platform he'd seen, visiting his dad at work.

He handed her the spike.

Shouldn't he do it? It was his dad who was the neurosurgeon.

He forced the spike into her fist because it was her stupid theory that the dog still had a brain. Classic boy. Horrible.

The dog's eye wasn't really there anymore. Andromeda winced and lined up the spike with the eye pit. The dog was so dead that it didn't take more than one whack on the end of the spike with a high-heeled shoe to send in the point clean.

The question of whether a brain remained had to be abandoned —just then, Spike's mom pulled in.

The best place to hide the dog was in Spike's sister's room. That was Andromeda's idea, and Spike was so flustered, he agreed. He would've done anything, so long as she helped him get the moldy dead dog off the dining room table.

Up to his sister's room went the dog in its puddle of alley wet. Andromeda split, and he got blamed, and it spread around school, and he was Spike ever since.

"You're the one who drove the spike," he tells her, his voice turned aside. "Spike."

She tap-dances away from him free—no zombie dog nor furious mom on her conscience.

"Hey, are you coming tonight?" His voice is back at the hole.

Most everything unties itself and drifts away. He's the one thing that, even if pushed, keeps coming back.

She goes to the fence and peers through the chink.

"You coming to the dance?" His face is tilted sideways, like hers, like in Claudio's kiss in *Much Ado About Nothing*.

"I don't have a dad to go with me."

"You have a grandmother," says Spike.

"You want me to dance with Grandmother? No thanks. Everyone else will have dads."

As if on cue, the back door opens. Grandmother steps out and hollers in French.

The words strike hard, and Andromeda wishes she didn't know French. French is a beautiful language, but on Grandmother's lips, every syllable is a verdict. So nice, would it be, to say *Je ne sais pas*, like Spike can.

She yells back at Grandmother beautifully.

Grandmother, muttering, slams the back door.

"What did she say?" Spike asks.

"I'm to go in and pack. My bus leaves late tonight."

He disappears from the hole and is suddenly stepping to the unlocked gate. And then he's swinging wide the gate and pushing clear the string of lights.

"One last dance."

"The bus," she says, letting him pull her. "I can't."

'But—a dance," he says, hanging onto her, running. "What else could save you?"

"With no dad, I won't get in."

He draws her on. "Trust me."

They cut from the street to the alley—a clear shot to the center of the city.

They slow before the dumpster where they found the dead dog.

She crouches, catching her breath.

As she watches the sky settle into a golden sunset, she finds that tears can't come.

He settles onto the ground between her and the stained place where the dog was. "I don't get why she's making you go."

Andromeda shrugs. "I'm an at-risk girl."

"What does that even mean?"

She wipes her eyes, not for any tears. Just because. "Grandmother says if I stay, I won't have chances."

"Chances for what?"

"I don't know."

Spike meanders the alleyway, kicking stones, hands in his pockets, staring back the way they came. He's probably wanting to go home.

"Are you going to forget me?" Andromeda calls.

His gaze catches on the dog stain. "How could I?"

She hugs her legs. "The kids there are going to be awful."

"We don't know that. Maybe they'll love you."

"Boarding houses for at-risk girls don't allow love. Or dancing."

He comes to her, draws his hands from his pockets. "Let's get you a dad."

"What dad?"

He takes her hand. "Mine."

"Your dad, the brain surgeon?" He was as pleasing a dad as could be, but—"There's no way he'd go for just me. I mean, would you?"

He tugs her to her feet.

They rush the alley corridor until it deposits them behind the city hospital.

He leads her through a back door where laundry is handled. Then down long white corridors, and up up up stairs.

They run, skirting bustling workstations. They skid before a broad door. *Neurosurgery*.

"This is it." He pulls her toward it.

She's breathless, but now is no time for catching breath.

The door to the operating theater opens, and there stands Spike's dad, garbed in surgical green, leaning over an operating table (exactly the size of a dining room table).

He puts down a railroad spike and turns toward her.

His eyes—the only bit of his face visible behind the mask—smile. "You made it."

He's the most handsome dad that could be. It leaves her delirious. He pulls off his mask.

She can't draw her eyes off him. "You don't have to come with me."

He's peeling off his gloves and discarding them on a tray a nurse holds. "Of course I'm coming with you."

There's sheer happiness in believing that something's terribly wrong, then realizing it's not.

The walk to the recital hall is silent and moonlit, her hand held by a dad.

They reach the doorway, strung with twinkle lights. The women selling tickets take one look at such a dad and step aside. They don't even make him pay.

He has all the moves. They dance all the ways she knows how. He's good, but she's better, and he knows it.

His face steams, then smokes. A storm wind sweeps in.

She keeps dancing.

His clothes blow to pieces. And there he goes with them, tearing apart at the seams until he's a lump of rags that she's dancing around. Dancing, though everyone's staring. Dancing, though Blunder's stopped singing. Dancing, despite that she's stuck inside the bus between an old man and the window.

Dancing, though the wheels start their turning. Dancing, though the bus is pitch dark but for racing lights striping the aisle—lights tracing exits (which aren't exits), little lights glaring at her not to cross them.

Dancing, though the sun's set and a boarding school machine will forever divide her from the night that a dad took her hand.

Dancing as stars light and follow—thousands of spotlights, eyes searching for her in the dark.

2

THE BUS EJECTS Andromeda onto the pavement before a gargantuan school. This isn't any city that she could attach to. This isn't Messina. This isn't Paris. Nor is it anything close to what she'd call a home.

This is Villa Golgotha.

She lifts her suitcase and stands back as the bus pulls away, leaving her confronting…

Gothic spires. Oaken doors leading to vast chambers stinking—even from here—of blood and smoke drifting from sacrifice tables. Children with faces like hogs peering down through sharp-pinnacled boarding school windows.

"Blunder," she whispers. "Where are you?"

Her hand clenches. Unclenches. The space surrounding it feels cold—no one there to hold on to her fingers. Not even the creature Blunder, who melted into tears after Grandmother forced a promise that she'd leave him behind.

Lightning cracks from a sweeping storm, casting a shattered white web behind Villa Golgotha.

"I can't do this."

But the last thing Spike's dad said to her was—"Give those kids a chance. How could they not love you?"

She shakes her head, chasing the storm.

The girls here might be fine. The teachers might smile.

Though, it's a crime that they don't allow dancing.

She crosses the lawn and approaches the boarding school beneath a cover of rainy-day birdsong.

Inside the front door, a foyer stretches bright and high, its floor polished.

Looking at her feet, she sees not the tiles beneath, sounding with the steps of robed teachers. Rather, she sees herself perfectly reflected, as though imprinted on the surface of a still lake.

Herself—idyllic in the moonflower summer dress that Grandmother said made her seem likeable.

And flowing out of the dress' tulle—toned dancer's legs.

She points her toe.

Her shoe meets the mirror girl's shoe—shinier than even the floor. On the soles of these shoes rests her secret, which will not keep. Metal plates made for tapping.

It's not tap dancing, *per se*, if it's just unfortunately loud shoes.

Or so she tells the headmistress, who has the face of a witch and, glaring down, seems even more put out than Grandmother. The headmistress holds out her hand for the shoes.

Andromeda's reflection apparently remains in concord with her own position—for the reflected little girl staring up from the floor tiles is smiling.

Perhaps she should comply, though, and give up the shoes. Her job, Grandmother said in her faux posh way, is to "fabricate a favorable impression."

But she can't give them up. They're her shoes!

She locks eyes with the little girl reflected, taking raps on the knuckles for obstinance.

3

The next day—a bright-dawning Sunday—looks promising. Moving alone through the egg-steamy breakfast hall isn't too bad.

Andromeda collects not-friendly-but-not-quite-unfriendly stares from the girls.

They don't bear the faces of hogs anymore.

They're just girls.

She moves into the breakfast line, in the center of the great hall. Glide—Spin—Reach.

She takes a tray. Glide—Spin—Reach.

Some of the girls, watching her, stop their eating. Glide—Spin—Reach.

A tall girl approaches.

Now everyone's watching.

No piggish nose studs the face of this girl. No tusks. Her smile looks like a model's.

She's one of the older girls. A ruler of this realm, maybe.

The children she passes cast looks that seem either respectful or pandering; looks that betray a shared secret, perhaps. Or maybe it's worship.

When the tall girl reaches her, Andromeda takes down her arms from fifth position. It's just as well. Her shoulders were tending tired.

The girl hands Andromeda a Dum Dum sucker. Root beer. "Welcome to Villa Golgotha."

Andromeda studies the sucker. "I've never felt right about how these are packaged." She winks, eyeing the sucker's wrinkly paper. "Suckers always look loosely covered."

And indeed, on this one, the twist on the top barely holds.

"People say it's fine, but that's difficult to accept, isn't it?" Andromeda asks. "Wetness always gets in and makes the wrapper too sticky."

She sniffs the sucker, which smells deliciously of root beer and… something else. "It's impossible to get at only the good stuff. One always winds up eating paper."

When Andromeda looks up, the tall girl isn't smiling. She's hating.

"It's just like I told them." The girl's teeth lengthen into pig tusks. "You're weird."

Andromeda peels away the wrapper to find, no root beer sucker —but a snail, impaled on a candy stick.

Andromeda surveys the horde of girls watching. She reads them.

They want her to scream. She's supposed to scream, in fact. Scream, and they'll begin the slow process of liking her.

Even the teachers won't mind if she screams. Screaming is the first step, for it's an admission—

She is weird. And she should show that she knows it. She should admit an aspiration to be like the girl standing before her, even if she can't dream of possessing that brand of beauty. She should proclaim that she's ashamed of herself, as she is; that she aims to unite with the collective.

Andromeda's expected to scream because it is truly upsetting, right? The snail on a stick in her hand exposes her weirdness, and she must acknowledge it. For she's juxtaposed against this greatness—this queen—standing before her; this model-quality girl whose nose is going squatty.

The queen glances around at the others—hundreds of girls, every one of them staring.

Their expressions reflect the queen's bliss.

The queen focuses on Andromeda. Raises her brow in a prompting way.

To scream would be to accept the fixed place that's been assigned by this queen, holding a powerful position in Villa Golgotha. The place she's offering Andromeda is low, granted, but still—it's a place.

"Well?" The piggy queen taps her hip.

Scream, and the hierarchy hums.

Like a row of Russian nesting dolls, every girl is ascribed her right place.

Those in the company of the queen at the top—the big dolls, the elite—will mock Andromeda before devouring her. They'll loathe her. Laugh at her.

It's expected.

Those at the hierarchy's middle—the medium-sized dolls, the snobs—they'll tolerate Andromeda as long as she charms them, as long as she lets them stand on her back.

The girls at the bottom tier—those tiny dolls creeping with Andromeda low over the earth—they're the jackals. They'll pretend to pity her until the moment comes when they've grown impoverished enough to eat one of their own. Or they'll try to build up comradery based on a mutual vehemence for oppressors. Uprisings will be planned, which will feel like friendship, but they never will happen.

Some of the low-ranking girls shall be elevated by beauty nascent in them now. Or applied beauty. It really doesn't matter. Girls set on the upward-tending conveyer belts in the machine are ready to be lied to.

The snobs will reward the bottom-dwellers, and some of the lowest girls will rise to the middle heights. Some, even, on the coattails of the queen, will sail to join the lofty elite to serve as scapegoats. Fans. Footstools. That's the most for which a bottom-tier girl can hope.

The queen stares at Andromeda with a look that seems like it really could kill.

The hall around them holds silence, crystalized. Every pig eye is fixed on Andromeda, gripping the candy stick spearing a snail.

"The caste system is dead." Andromeda places the snail in her mouth.

The dining hall bursts with immaculate screams!

The queen's mouth gapes. She seems to want to flee, but she stands frozen, staring.

On Andromeda's tongue—a stirring.

The snail wasn't hurt by the candy stick, then. Only chased.

In the dark closeness of her mouth, it must feel safe.

The queen's eyes widen as Andromeda opens her mouth, revealing the snail's body lengthening.

Its stalked eyes tap her upper lip like the fingers of one blind, trying to make out a face.

The queen turns an ugly white, then dry heaves. She lets an extraordinary belch. She turns herself inside out—prostrates on knees and hands before pancakes, liquefied on the floor.

Andromeda lets the snail crawl from her tongue onto the back of her hand.

She flash-mob-dances out to let it go in the garden.

No one follows.

4

Days and nights wheel, the sun and moon the hands of a clock, spinning hours like seeds and setting them one by one into flight.

The girls keep a collective eye on Andromeda. The teachers, docile, straight-jacketed by robes, see nothing.

"It's difficult," Andromeda whispers when she's alone, to Blunder, wherever he is. "I wish you'd come back."

It's unclear how creatures communicate, but sometimes she feels he can hear her.

Andromeda stands on a bridge flanking the school—it's as far as she's allowed to walk on her own.

But its far enough.

She can scarcely make out the spires of Villa Golgotha above the downtown shops.

It's a year to the day from the night that a dad took her hand— and tonight, that dad's coming. He and Spike will arrive soon for a visit.

She told them she was fine, not to come. But they wouldn't listen.

After this night, she'll no longer be fine, though. For after they visit, she'll lose them. Again.

She watches the sunset light the water and wishes that it might not fade. Every bit of orange, of red seeping into the sun, brings Spike and his dad nearer. And every bit of indigo slipping into the west quickens the moment they'll leave.

The evening's a clear one. The moon rises, a white stone in the darkening eastern sky. It lays soft on the face of the river running under the bridge.

The moon's shape is cocoon-like. It's a waxing gibbous—partial but swelling and soon to blow full. Winking one eye, she can make out the thread that suspends it.

She reaches, collecting strands of its light among her fingers until it drapes booey and melted.

"How cool you are," she whispers, turning moonlight over and over in her hands. "Silky as clouds. Solid as earth."

A little more plying, and the light takes the consistency of wet clay.

She shapes it into a heart. Not a simpering valentine mock heart, but one human.

She takes care in creating it—anatomically sound, inside and out.

Four chambers, each stabling one horse of the apocalypse. Four chambers harboring one of the four winds, channeling all weathers. Four chambers, each an empty bedroom she's left. Four chambers, each holding one letter: B—L—U—E.

Headlights break the twilight. Sly, sharp headlights. Brilliant.

She moves to the sidewalk edging the bridge.

From the front seats of the car, Spike and his dad both catch her glance. They cast genuine, seeing, kind-hearted, non-piggish smiles.

Andromeda strains to glimpse into the backseat, behind them.

There, a thing stirs.

Spike's dad pulls over. The car's back door swings.

And out spills the creature Blunder.

Blunder fights the moonlight to reach her. Stars like spears glance off his blue scales.

He races to standing before her and sinks his teeth into her leg. He means well, though.

And then she's in their arms. Spike holds her so close that his jacket cloaks her. A skin.

Everything shimmers as she presses her forehead against the soft edge of his dad's neck—a place magical enough to set babies to sleep.

"You really came," she whispers.

"Of course we came." Spike's dad straightens.

He draws away.

He watches over Spike and Andromeda, not like the head-mistress, but like the moon—steady and always—as the two of them sit on the brink of the bridge, peering together at the water ripples, beating like the pulse of a pendulum.

Down the street, a restaurant pipes music. Blunder stands beside them, singing along—a serenade to people lost in the romance of love.

"Shush." She sets her finger against Blunder's mouth.

The love resting in Andromeda for Spike is the love between brothers. Gamey, not sweet. Safe love. Honest. Not love as a toy. Not bitter love, forced, as by pressing an unripe fruit.

Spike studies the water slipping under the bridge. "Watch."

He casts in a dry leaf, still green, as though frozen in summer, which the current takes and spins.

She snatches another leaf. One good and brown and broad and bowed like the hull of a warship.

She casts it down beside his.

They race to the other side of the bridge and catch themselves on the rail.

They stare down at the water.

The leaves don't manifest. They're left looking at only themselves.

Their bodies, reflected, seem part of the water. Permanent. Painted there and bound to remain for all time.

Andromeda points her toe, feeling for the touch of her reflection. For his.

"Hey, are those tap shoes?" he asks.

She spins into an easy number and uptowns around him.

"They let you wear tap shoes?" He spins to keep sight of her. "I thought dancing, here, was forbidden."

"Mostly, they leave me alone." Andromeda stills and looks into the water.

Their leaves aren't coming. They've been snagged by something. Water eddies. Trolls. Trash.

The reflected stars wheel as though driven by witches.

The footsteps of Spike's dad, walking the length of the bridge, sound more beautiful than tap shoes. If only they'd never stop sounding.

Full night comes with a heaviness pressing, bringing Spike and Andromeda to their knees, facing each other.

A chilly breeze lifts from the water, shivering them as the moon arcs west over the bridge and drifts earthward.

"How are the kids here?" Spike asks. "And the teachers—are they nice?"

"I made you something." She opens her hand, and there stands the human heart comprised of clay from the moon.

He touches it. Traces its curves. "That's really cool."

She holds it out. "It's for you and your dad."

He rests his gaze on it, as though watching for it to beat. As though afraid that it might.

She holds it out further. "Take it."

"It's so cool, you should keep it." He stands, glancing back at his dad. "He's waving me over. That means it's getting late."

She eases to her feet. Heat and cold together bathe her as he walks away.

Blunder clings to her leg, his claws piercing.

She doesn't push him off. A little bloodletting about now feels right.

Spike's dad hugs her around the shoulders. He asks her something she can't understand. It's difficult to hear anything—not his voice, not the wind moving the water, not the ticking moon, not Blunder sniffling—for the chaos of grief billowing in her like fire.

Spike's dad goes on speaking. Something about how dark the night's growing. How unsafe. He urges her into the car.

She stares up until he comes into focus.

"There's a restaurant just down the street, right across from your school," he says. "Have you been there? They make wonderful sundaes. How about we share one, before we go?"

He doesn't get it. They're going to go. No matter what, they're going to go.

They stand before her like two pieces of free starry sky, bright and fresh above Villa Golgotha, transcending the grip of the machine.

Andromeda glances at the car's taillights.

At the thought of watching them fade, her blood boils.

Spike holds open the car door. "Please come."

Why, so she can twist under sorrow all over again in a minute? So she can crumble to ashes when this car, a dad's car, sly-eyed, so cool, dumps her on the doorstep of Villa Golgotha?

Standing here, facing off with them, they aren't leaving. It feels good.

But this can't go on forever.

"Rip off the bandage," she whispers. "Don't draw it out."

They don't move. They just watch her.

Better to be the one doing the leaving. Someone's got to be brave enough.

She beats it down the road toward the boarding school's spires, then cuts down a dark alley.

She runs, passing dumpsters and service doors, tears across side streets until she's good and lost. Well, she knows where she is, but there's no way they can track her.

She hides behind a brick building and peeks out. She can't help it. Seeing them one last time might be worth the pain.

There go red taillights.

It might be them, or it might not.

The taillights brighten as the car slows. They dim as the car picks up speed. Finally, they vanish.

Andromeda wanders between buildings until she reaches the edge of the river, beneath the bridge.

There, Blunder bobs to the surface.

The moon shimmers in the water—rippling, folding, distorting its craters, its curves.

She wades knee-deep in to reach Blunder.

As the sky ages, the wind lifts and handles the water more roughly, tearing the moon to shreds.

From under the bridge slips a green leaf—Spike's green leaf—caught in a cluster of waterborne weeds.

Andromeda waits, but her leaf does not follow.

White headlights swell the night brilliant.

Andromeda scrambles onto the bank. Blunder climbs out right behind her.

A car turns down the street and heads for the bridge.

Its headlights are sly. Bright. So cool.

They're back. They've come back.

She rushes up to the sidewalk on the bridge. At her side, Blunder bounds, roaring joy.

The car passes slowly.

It isn't Spike's dad.

It's a man.

A strange man. A strange man rolling down the window.

Andromeda backs off.

He stops. "Are you lost?"

She stares at him, staring at her.

He doesn't seem treacherous, but treacherous things often don't. Dum Dum suckers. Girls. Teachers. Lights. Sundaes.

Blunder paws at her leg, then flies off.

She races away behind him, but she's too spent to run far and must stop.

She glances back.

The car's idling.

It backs up and pauses near to her.

The man, from his window, watches.

On his face lies a mean tiny grin. His eyes, tracing her head to toe, calculate, like he's measuring how much trouble she's worth.

She draws out her heart made of moon.

The man calls, "I can give you a ride, if you want one."

She steadies her breathing. Winks one eye. Cocks the clay heart. Fires.

It strikes his red taillight, smashing it.

"What the hell?" The man gets out.

Blunder drags Andromeda into flight. Over waters they soar, wild waters.

Andromeda climbs through her boarding room window and tunnels under her covers. Blunder crams himself in her arms, trembling. She strokes his rough back, some scales sloughing off, until he quiets.

The moon, nearly touching the horizon now, takes on a glow as it peers through the window. It's the color of a campfire's reflection on flesh.

In the sky, hanging silent and flushed, it seems unveiled. Concrete. Fired clay, chipped and broken.

While living in Villa Golgotha, broken is something she can't let herself be. If she walks around broken at this boarding school, the machine will dismantle her.

As Blunder sleeps, she collects his loose scales.

One by one, she fixes them onto her body, plating her skin where it bleeds.

5

Andromeda, lightly scaled, moves through the halls of Villa Golgotha. Wearing blue scales feels a thousand times better than plain skin.

Blunder, beside her, is still mostly scaled. Just a few tender inches, here and there, shimmer with light.

For the first day donning this mask, Andromeda's gone easy— blue scales just over the eyes; some on the cheeks and hands. A row covering each ear.

Where the scales lay, there's no pain.

"Hey, weirdo," says the queen, in a friendly way that masterfully aims to wound without picking up any responsibility for the damage.

"Is it just me, or is she looking uglier these days?" the queen asks her entourage.

It doesn't even hurt. It just bounces right off.

"No wonder you've just had one visit in a whole year."

Okay, that one hurt.

Andromeda glances down. There, on the floor, lies a fallen blue scale.

The queen smiles, seeming pleased with the reward of a reaction. "I saw you on the bridge."

Andromeda looks up, the fire in her catching.

Her distress seems to send out a signal, a scent, keen to attract the elite. Then the snobs come, the scavengers, all gathering in a crowd.

"Who was that with you?" asks the queen. "And I saw you run off. Was that your boyfriend?"

More scales fall.

The queen closes in. "Did he throw you away, just like everyone has?"

People say words can't hurt, but these sear. They seep. It's as though Andromeda's absorbing a puddle of toxin.

"I'm sure he'll never visit you again," says the queen.

Andromeda clenches her fist.

The queen asks, "How does it feel, to be completely alone?"

In a rush of blue, Blunder leaps at the queen as Andromeda swings. Hard.

Something cracks when her fist strikes the queen's face. Andromeda hopes she's broken off a tusk or flattened that snout. A crooked nose might go some distance to civilize this one.

But from the agony throbbing, it's clear that the snap came from her own hand.

Watching the queen fleeing, blood dripping, feels like justice.

The crowd breaks into a stampede—girls smashing into each other. Girls screaming about blood. Screaming for it.

The headmistress witch breaks through the chaos.

Everyone stills. Everyone points.

The witch grabs Andromeda by the ear and drags her down the hall.

The girls back against the walls. None jump to Andromeda's defense. None say that it wasn't her fault.

But that doesn't matter. Blunder is galloping after her, his eyes piercing and full of plots. As well as she knows how to get into trouble, he knows how to get out of it.

In the headmistress's office, after the lecture—through which Andromeda stayed silent and pretended to care—she runs her fingers through Blunder's scales, loosening all that will fall.

It's difficult to do, with a bandaged, broken finger.

Blunder helps her, clawing off belly scales.

She lays them in rows, plating every inch of her skin.

Blunder gazes at her as though he's in love.

Catching a glimpse of herself in his shining eyes, she can no longer see any difference between herself and her creature.

6

THE NEXT DAY, as Andromeda moves about the school, the girls do stare—but they make way for her. No one laughs anymore. No one even speaks.

The queen, when she catches Andromeda's glance, skitters away.

The queen's moved on, it seems.

All day, she's gotten in the way of another bottom-rung girl —Rosaline.

Rosaline has zero potential, when viewed through the paradigm of the machine. Rosaline's plain looking. Average at everything. Completely unremarkable.

Andromeda watches the queen give Rosaline a hard time. Why is it that the people who dislike attention always seem to catch the most of it?

The queen seems fiercer today, darkened by that bruise on her face. She snatches Rosaline's books and throws them onto the floor.

Andromeda pushes between them.

"What are you going to do?" asks the queen. "Want to break your other hand?"

Andromeda tightens her fist, bandaged, yes, but now scaled.

"Touch me again, and you'll be thrown out on the street," says the queen.

"Touch Rosaline, and your face will be the next thing to break," says Andromeda.

It could be that the queen's afraid of her now. Or she might be disgusted by something so scaly. Whatever the reason, the queen backs off and leaves.

"You shouldn't have done that." Rosaline hurries to pick up her books. "She'll think you're my friend and get back at you worse for that squashed nose you gave her."

"Do you care what that queen thinks?" asks Andromeda.

"No," says Rosaline. "But I'd rather you keep the point you scored off her."

That sounded a little like friendship.

And—though Andromeda can't quite make out why, it felt so good to place her body between Rosaline and the queen.

She takes Rosaline's hand and breaks into a run.

"Where are we going?" asks Rosaline. "Class will start in a minute."

Andromeda pulls her around a corner, toward the foyer. "We have to figure out what to do about her."

"Why bother?" Rosaline jerks her hand out of Andromeda's. "If we manage to get her to leave us alone, she'll just move on to somebody else."

Andromeda shoves through the doors of the foyer.

Empty of people, the place looks enormous. It's full of light, the floor gleaming, the late afternoon sun shining in from a dozen high windows.

Rosaline follows her, though slowly. She seems to feel lost in a place so vast, so open.

Andromeda paces, Blunder right behind her. "It's the machine. The problem is the stupid machine."

"There's nothing we can do," says Rosaline.

"As long as it runs, it'll keep churning out people like her, like all of them. It'll keep trapping some of us down at the bottom." Andromeda paces the other way. "There's got to be a way to break it."

Rosaline makes herself yet smaller, crouching into a tight, brown-headed ball.

Andromeda studies herself, covered in scales. "This can't be the answer." She painfully pulls one off. "Shields only work 'till you lose them." She rubs her arms, knocking off all that will fall.

Rosaline just watches.

"Hurting her—it did nothing." She shakes her hand, its break throbbing.

"It doesn't matter what we do," says Rosaline. "There's nothing anyone can do."

Music from the restaurant across the street rises to life.

Andromeda opens the front door, sending slanted light glittering over the floor.

The music carries a wonderful beat. People at the restaurant are dancing.

"One last dance," Andromeda whispers.

Her throbbing hand warms with the memory of Spike's.

"What else could save us?" Andromeda whispers.

"People like her never change," says Rosaline. "It's the nature of things."

Andromeda props open the front door. "The machine was made with human hands. Such hands never could break it."

"Look, thanks for scaring her off, but this problem has no solution." Rosaline stands. "The bell's rung for class. We should go."

Andromeda stares out the front door, at the restaurant, at the people, at the late afternoon shimmering with music.

"Something higher might break it." She turns and holds Rosaline's gaze.

Rosaline's eyes widen as Andromeda sets into a folk swing dance.

The music is perfect. Strong downbeats. Nice high points. Plenty of structure for improvisation.

Rosaline whispers, "What do think you're doing?" She checks the hallway, from where hundreds of girls are about to wend in, crossing the foyer to their classrooms.

"This is an old dance from Asia," says Andromeda. "It's brilliant."

The scales that she didn't chase fall right off. The fire in her lifts and dissipates into mist. Grief sinks away through the soles of her shoes.

Andromeda reaches for Rosaline. "Dance with me."

The smile spreading on Rosaline's face betrays that she wants to.

Andromeda takes Rosaline's hands and reduces the dance to a series of four simple motions.

Rosaline follows. She picks it up quick.

"All right." Andromeda lays more complex moves around her.

Rosaline keeps with the four steps—a peddle tone for Andromeda to create what's winding up as sensational choreography.

Girls drift in slowly. Girls staring. Teachers, too.

Andromeda doesn't dream of stopping. Neither does Rosaline. In fact, Rosaline picks up some of the complex stuff. She's good. Really good, actually.

Around them, girls close in. They glance at the teachers, waiting for someone to stop this.

Nobody stops this.

Everyone just holds still, serving witness to the star-studded moment, when two girls pound to pieces the structure of Villa Golgotha.

"Enough!" The headmistress slams the front door.

The music strangles.

The voice of the headmistress carries power and manages to stop their feet dancing. But not their hearts racing. Not their lungs drawing air that tastes of adrenaline. Not their eyes meeting each other and knowing they've found a way to dismantle the machine.

"I've had it." The headmistress beelines for Andromeda.

A girl, her gaze locked on Andromeda, swings the door open wide.

The headmistress leers down. "This is the last time—" But a new song chokes her words.

The new song thumps upbeat and faster.

Perfection.

Andromeda rocks, side to side. She catches the eyes of as many girls as she can. Even some of the teachers.

Their gazes, like threads, interconnect.

Rosaline stands by Andromeda. Joins her. And then more girls rock, side to side.

Andromeda struts into what might look easy, but she lets her steps syncopate.

The girls, entranced, stare.

Andromeda leads them—again, simple steps.

Many follow.

Even some of the teachers join in. Blunder's so bad a dancer, he's wonderful.

"Stop it," shouts the headmistress. "I said stop it!"

Nobody heeds her. They can hardly hear her.

The headmistress snatches Andromeda's ear and jerks her away.

It hurts, but it doesn't. She's got a protection far better than scales.

As the headmistress hauls her, Andromeda catches a final glimpse of the foyer.

There, the girls, all bright, seem changed. Some of them watch her with eyes full of joy. Their stares feel like bridges.

"Pure art," Andromeda whispers.

Creativity, dance, artistry—these are greater than any machine of oppression. Whatever comes next, this insight, this superpower, will stand at the ready.

Just before they reach the headmistress's office—a blood-curdling creak peals.

Engines rake and slam. Gears grind and roll. Metal whines as it bends…

…and there goes the machine.

THE END

*Thank you
to my family, who has loved me,
who taught me how to dance.*

FREE EBOOK

Eight-year-old Swift is lost in dreams of sea legends and pirate adventures, until an encounter with the deadly power of the ocean shocks him into reality. Swift struggles to hang onto his childhood fantasies, but his new understanding of the fragile nature of life and friendships threatens to swamp his hope.

Under the guidance of his older brother, Caius, Swift must learn to brave the challenging waves of change without losing himself to their destruction.

ALSO BY TRICIA D. WAGNER

A STARRY-EYED BOY. A CRYPTIC MAP. A MYTHICAL TREASURE. WHAT PERILS AWAIT IN THE CHASING OF DREAMS?

As Swift lives up to his name and his family legacy, young adults receive a fast-paced fantasy that will appeal not just on the adventure or fantasy levels, but in matters of the heart as the young struggle for independence and action in the face of parental restrictions. Tricia D. Wagner's attention to pairing psychological struggle with the adventure of finding a promised treasure creates a story that pulls on the emotions of young readers as it satisfies their desire for action and adventure.

-D. Donovan, Senior Reviewer, Midwest Book Review

WHERE FISH CAN BREATHE

TEN-YEAR-OLD SWIFT LONGS TO BE AS GROWN UP AS HIS BROTHERS, BUT CONFRONTING HIMSELF IN THE WILDS OF THE NORTH ATLANTIC, HE MUST CONTEND WITH WHAT IT MEANS TO BE A MAN.

SEA OF GLASS

WHEN AN OLD ANGLER PRESSES TEO TO SEEK A GODDESS—THE SEA ANGEL—FOR RESCUE, TEO SETS OUT ALONG BAJA'S WILD COAST TO TEST WHETHER HELP CAN BE FOUND AT THE HANDS OF THE GODS.

TO LEARN THE TRUTH, HE MUST LOOK BEYOND LEGENDS AND SUMMON THE COURAGE TO CHALLENGE HIS PAPÁ.

AND TO REACH FREEDOM, HE MUST TAP HIS OWN STRENGTH, HIDDEN BENEATH WOUNDS LAID BY GLASS.

ABOUT THE AUTHOR

TRICIA D. WAGNER IS AN AWARD-WINNING NOVELIST, POET, AND SHORT STORY WRITER. SHE GREW UP IN AMARILLO, TEXAS, CHASING STORMS, RIDING STALLIONS, SOJOURNING THROUGH PAINTED CANYONS, DISAPPEARING INTO FLOATING MESAS UNDER STARRY SKIES.

SHE NOW LIVES IN ROCKFORD, ILLINOIS (THOUGH THE TRUTH IS, SHE'S A CITIZEN OF A DOZEN FICTIONAL COUNTRIES.) TRICIA WORKS IN EDUCATION AND LIVES DAY TO DAY WONDERSTRUCK BUT LUCKILY CAN FEEL HER WAY ABOUT THIS TERRIFYING, BEAUTIFUL EARTH THROUGH WRITING.

TRICIA HAS PIECES PUBLISHED IN THE *WRITE CITY MAGAZINE*, *CHICAGO NEWA*, *WORD OF ART 3D*, *LITERARY YARD*, AND *MIDWEST REVIEW*.

AUTHOR'S NOTE

I love connecting with readers and writers. If, you're interested in stories, then you're a kindred spirit to me, and I have lots more in store for you.

To quote another kindred spirit in writing, Jedi Master Stephen King:

"Writing is magic, as much as the water of life as any other art. The water is free. So drink. Drink and be filled up."

If you're interested not only in stories, but in story creation, visit my website and sign up to receive a **FREE Story Kickoff Character Worksheet.**

I designed this tool for that first moment of getting our feet wet at the brink of a story.

To get your FREE worksheet, visit:
www.TriciaWagner.com